For Marylène, Rafaël and Lucille,
Suzi, Jamie, George and Freddie.
And for Mum x

BLOOMSBURY CHILDREN'S BOOKS
Bloomsbury Publishing Plc
50 Bedford Square, London, WC1B 3DP, UK

BLOOMSBURY, BLOOMSBURY CHILDREN'S BOOKS
and the Diana logo are trademarks of Bloomsbury Publishing Plc

First published in Great Britain 2019 by Bloomsbury Publishing Plc

A catalogue record for this book is available from the British Library

ISBN 978 1 4088 9292 3 (HB)

2 4 6 8 10 9 7 5 3 1

Printed in China by Leo Paper Products, Heshan, Guangdong

All papers used by Bloomsbury Publishing Plc are natural, recyclable products from
wood grown in well managed forests. The manufacturing processes conform to
the environmental regulations of the country of origin.

To find out more about our authors and books visit www.bloomsbury.com
and sign up for our newsletters

CHRIS NAYLOR-BALLESTEROS

The Lonely CHRISTMAS TREE

BLOOMSBURY

LONDON OXFORD NEW YORK NEW DELHI SYDNEY

'Twas the night before Christmas,

and high on a hill,

a lonely tree shivered

in the cold and the still.

The tree was once part
of a huge forest home,
but those days were gone –
now it stood all alone.

Other trees nestled

all snug and aglow,

while the lonely tree dreamt

of the magic below.

And perched on its hillside,

no company to keep,

the tree settled down

for a long winter's sleep.

When suddenly – oh! –

through the frosted-breath night

came the crunching of footsteps

and a warm beam of light.

And soon the tree fell

in midwinter's glow,

then landed abreast

of the new-fallen snow.

Then away through the night

went a fellow so jolly!

Trudging through mistletoe,

ivy and holly.

And then in a twinkling,

that stranger so dear,

set straight to his work

to spread goodwill and cheer.

He spoke not a word

but with effortless grace,

made the tree a new home

in a happier place.

And bestowed at the top

the gift of a star,

which brought new companions

from near and afar.

The tree how it glistened,

no longer alone,

was back with old friends

and finally home.

Then St Nicholas called,

ere he flew out of sight . . .

"Happy Christmas to all,

and to all

a good night!"